First published 2008 by
A & C Black Publishers Ltd
38 Soho Square, London, W1D 3HB

www.acblack.com

Text copyright © 2008 Rob Childs
Illustrations copyright © 2008 Pam Smy

The rights of Rob Childs and Pam Smy to be
identified as the author and illustrator of this work respectively
have been asserted by them in accordance with the
Copyrights, Designs and Patents Act 1988.

ISBN: 978-0-7136-8962-4

A CIP catalogue for this book is available from the British Library.

This book is produced using paper that is made from wood grown in
managed, sustainable forests. It is natural, renewable and recyclable.
The logging and manufacturing processes conform to the
environmental regulations of the country of origin.

Printed and bound in Great Britain by
CPI Cox & Wyman, Reading, RG1 8EX

B.A.S.E.
CAMP

Rob Childs
Illustrated by Pam Smy

A & C Black • London

4734282

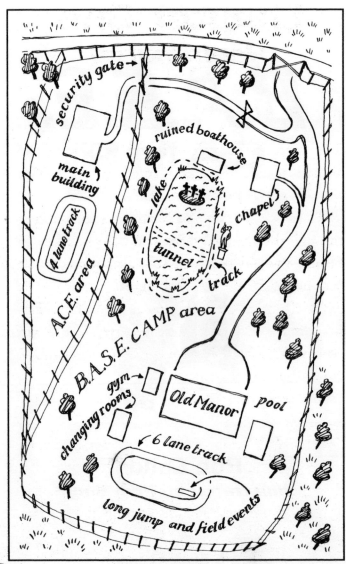

security gate →

main building ↗

ruined boathouse →

A.C.E. area

4 lane track

lake

tunnel

chapel

track

B.A.S.E. CAMP area

gym →

changing rooms ↗

Old Manor

pool

6 lane track

long jump and field events

Chapter One
Roommates

The green, vintage Bentley purred along the avenue of oak trees and scrunched to a halt in the wet gravel of the courtyard.

'Here we are, m'boy,' Gramps said, peering through the rain-spattered windscreen. 'Hard to believe my old boarding school is going to be *your* home for the next fortnight.'

Gareth stared at the ancient building. The skyline was dominated by its towers and tall chimneys, which pointed up into the dark clouds like bony fingers.

'Bet you never thought you'd see this place again, eh, Gramps?'

'Aye, you're right there, m'boy,' Gramps said, nodding. 'The Old Manor hasn't changed a bit though, by the look of it, in the past 50 years.'

'The name has,' Gareth reminded him. 'It's now known as B.A.S.E. Camp – the British Academy of Sporting Excellence.'

'Aye, well,' Gramps sighed. 'It'll always be the Old Manor to me – the haunted house!'

Gareth laughed. 'Most of the tales about your schooldays are ghost stories.'

They climbed out of the car, and Gareth collected his bags from the boot. 'Sure you won't stay for a while, Gramps?' he asked, suddenly feeling nervous. 'Y'know, have a little look round, like.'

'No, that can wait till the weekend when I come with your mother for the Open Day,' said Gramps. 'You're about to meet a whole new bunch of pals, so I won't hang around and get in your way.'

'OK then. Thanks for bringing me. I'll look forward to telling you everything on Sunday.'

Gramps slipped his grandson a wink. 'Aye, well, perhaps not *everything*, eh?' he chuckled. 'Best to keep mum, as they say, about any of them ghosts you might meet!'

When Gramps left to drive home through the afternoon traffic, Gareth was shown into one of the small dormitories on the second floor. Only the top bed of one of the two bunks had not already been claimed.

'Good job I don't mind heights,' he said, grinning. 'I'm a high jumper.'

A drawled response came from the opposite top bunk.

'Yeah? Well don't go jumpin' out of bed and makin' a noise in the middle of the night, man. I'm a light sleeper.'

A long, black leg trailed over the side of the bunk, dangling down in front of the face of the boy below, who was perched on the edge of the bed. He pushed it away and went on tightening the spikes in his running shoes. 'You've got smelly feet,' he complained.

'Not my feet, man – just my socks.'

'Same thing.'

'I'm Gareth, by the way,' said Gareth, interrupting his roommates. 'What events do you two do?'

The lad in the top bunk sat up and pulled on a pair of trainers. 'Adam – long jump and sprints,' he said and then pointed downwards. 'That's Wonder Boy, who says he's a runner.'

'Wonder Boy?'

'Yeah. Ever since he got here, he's not stopped *wonderin'* about stuff.'

'Most people call me Eddie,' the boy on the bottom bunk put in. 'I only said "I wonder who's sharing this room with us".'

'And wonder what we're doin' later. And what's for tea. And…'

'OK, OK,' Eddie sighed. 'Sorry – guess I'm just a bit nervous.'

'We all are,' Gareth said in support. 'What *are* we doing, anyway, this afternoon?'

'Whatever they say, man,' grunted Adam.

'Who's *they*?'

'The coaches.'

'Adam was here at Easter, too,' Eddie explained, pulling a face. 'Been boasting how not many people get invited back for extra coaching in the summer.'

'Perhaps he needs it,' Gareth grinned.

'We *all* need it, man. These guys are the best coaches around,' said Adam, and then added, 'Well, at least that's what they say.'

Gareth smiled and hoisted one of his bags onto the bunk. 'So who's got the bed below me?' he asked, looking at the bulging leather case that had been left there to claim it.

'Dunno,' said Adam. 'But if he can lug that great thing around with him, I reckon he must be a thrower. Y'know, big solid kid − strong in the arm and thick in the head!' He began to climb down from his bunk and trod on Eddie's coat, which lay across the pillow. There was the distinct sound of something snapping.

'Oops! What was that?'

Eddie put a hand in one of the pockets and pulled out a broken pair of sunglasses. 'Just as well I'm not going to need them in this weather,' he murmured.

At that moment, another boy appeared in the doorway, almost filling the space.

'See the gang's all here at last,' he said, strolling into the room. 'Name's Tom.'

'Where've you been hidin', man?' Adam asked him.

'Nowhere, *man*,' Tom responded in kind. 'Just having a bit of a snoop around. Then I met some bloke with white hair on the top floor, who told me it was private.'

'Who was that?' demanded Adam, suddenly serious.

Tom shrugged. 'No idea. He obviously wasn't one of the coaches.'

'Why not?'

'Too old and scruffy.'

'Look who's asking all the questions now,' said Eddie, surprised that Adam seemed so interested. 'He's probably just the caretaker.'

Tom grinned. 'Ought to start taking more care of himself, then. He needed a shave and was wearing some tatty cardigan with holes in it.'

'So what did you do?' asked Gareth.

'I cleared off before he could report me,' Tom said, opening his case. 'And when I glanced back, he'd gone.'

Gareth laughed. 'Sounds like he could be one of my grandad's ghosts.'

'What?'

'Long story. I'll explain later.'

Adam grabbed his sports bag off the bunk and made for the door. 'C'mon, you guys, time to go. Last one out the changin' room has to clean it up.'

'First I've heard about that,' Eddie complained, gathering up his own kit.

'Tons of things they don't tell yer here, Wonder Boy. You have to learn to look after number one at B.A.S.E. Camp.'

Chapter Two
Golden Goals

'Right, you lot! Time for action, not words,' boomed the voice of the head coach above the noise in the changing room. 'You're going out for a run.'

A hush fell over the group of young athletes. Each had been given a baggy, white vest to wear, but Tom was finding it uncomfortably tight. He tried to conceal his bulges by not tucking it into his shorts.

'But it's still raining... Coach,' he said, just remembering to add the expected title. 'Can't we train inside?'

The man stroked his beard thoughtfully while he looked Tom up and down. He did not seem impressed by what he saw. 'So, it's wet. What's wrong with that, laddie?' he sneered.

'Nothing, Coach, but why...'

Tom's protests were cut short.

'No *buts* at B.A.S.E. Camp. You do what

you're told – and you do it quick.'

The boys were in no position to argue – and nor did they want to. They knew how privileged they were to have been chosen to attend the Academy. It meant they were seen as potential future stars of athletics.

'Not a good start, man,' said Adam, as they all jostled into position by the door. 'It's only Monday and Blackbeard's already got you marked down as a troublemaker.'

Tom gave a shrug. 'I was just going to ask why we don't wait till it stops raining.'

'They don't like questions here,' Adam told him. 'And *you* might not like the answers.'

In preparation for the cross-country run, the boys were put through a series of warm-up exercises that soon had everyone breathing heavily.

'Phew!' gasped Tom during a brief lull in the activities. 'I'm not really built for all this bending and stretching lark.'

'I can see that,' Adam grinned, poking Tom's stomach. 'Still, you might be gettin' some practice at throwin' soon.'

'How d'you mean?'

'Throwin' up!'

Adam was right. Tom was sick behind a tree before he had covered the first mile of the course through the woods.

'Must've had too much for lunch,' he groaned, leaning against the trunk for support.

Adam and Gareth were content to jog along in the main bunch of mud-spattered boys, but Eddie was setting a hot pace out in front by himself. He loved running and had two trophies at home from county and national cross-country championships as proof of his speed and stamina.

After leaving the woods, Eddie stretched his lead along the driveway and checked over his shoulder to see the next runner just emerging from the trees.

'Never mind him!' came a shout from one of the coaches, who chugged across the grass towards him on a motorised buggy. 'What's your name?'

'Eddie, Coach.'

'Surname.'

'Peters, Coach.'

'Make for the lake, Peters, and turn left at the statue.'

The buggy veered off so that the coach could

yell some advice at the others now pounding along the road.

Eddie saw that the path forked by the statue and he slowed to make sure he went in the right direction – in this case, to his left. He often got his left and right mixed up.

Once on the well-beaten track around the lake, Eddie relaxed a little and noticed there was a small island with a number of white crosses beneath a clump of trees.

'Strange place for a cemetery,' he murmured.

Eddie had no more time to take in the scenery. Another backward glance showed him that his nearest rival was making something of a charge and had managed to close the gap between them. He smiled grimly to himself, confident that he had enough energy to hold off any challenge.

'He'll have nothing left for the finish, the rate he's going.'

Eddie passed a ramshackle boathouse and he could now see a small chapel almost hidden by a screen of oak trees. From there, they had been told to head back up the drive, cross the courtyard and wait by the outdoor swimming pool near the house.

As the two runners left the lake area, Eddie was about to go round the back of the chapel when he heard a cry from behind.

'Hey! Wrong way. We turn right here.'

Eddie faltered, allowing a hint of doubt to enter his mind, but he carried on.

'Suit yourself,' came the cackle. 'See ya!'

'Sure this was the way they said,' Eddie muttered, coming to a halt.

Reluctantly, he doubled back and went round the other side of the chapel instead. He found himself on a narrow path through the oaks, but when he emerged onto the winding driveway, the new leader was out of sight.

Eddie cursed. 'I'll never catch him now.'

By the time he reached the swimming pool, however, the only person there was Blackbeard. The head coach did not look best pleased.

'Reckoned you could cheat, did you, Peters?' he growled.

'Cheat?' Eddie gasped, trying to swallow his disappointment at being beaten.

'Aye, cheat! Taking that short cut past the chapel.'

'B… but I was just following that other kid, Coach,' he protested.

'What other kid?' thundered Blackbeard, grabbing Eddie by the arm. 'You know what we do with cheats here, laddie?'

'I'm not a...'

'We give them a bath!'

Almost before Eddie realised what was meant by the threat, he found himself lifted off the ground, carried several metres to the pool and then dumped into the water.

It was shockingly cold. As his head broke the surface, he choked out some water and saw Blackbeard looming over him.

'And you'll stay in there, Peters, till everybody gets back. I want them to see how we deal with cheats at B.A.S.E. Camp.'

'Just as well you can swim,' said Tom, making the bed creak as he sat next to Eddie, who was huddled inside a blanket and sipping at a mug of tea.

Adam leant over the edge of the bunk above. 'Everybody can swim, man.'

'I can't,' Tom confessed.

'Well, you don't need to worry,' Adam chuckled. 'Bet Blackbeard couldn't even pick you up!'

'Ha ha! Very funny!' Tom scowled. 'You ought to be on TV.'

'Will be when I'm rich and famous.'

Adam dropped down onto the floor and looked out of the window to see Blackbeard talking with another coach in the courtyard. He recognised the bald head from the Easter course, and gave a groan.

'What's the matter?' asked Gareth.

'Just spotted someone I'd hoped wouldn't still be here. A little French coach we nicknamed *Petit Pierre*. He's a right sadist in the gym.'

'Don't let your tea get cold, Eddie,' said Tom, changing the subject. He didn't much like the sound of Petit Pierre.

Eddie screwed up his face. 'It tastes worse than the water in the pool.'

'Can't be as bad as the fruit juice we get given,' Adam told them. 'Pity old Tom-Tom took two hours to finish the course – you wouldn't have had to stay in there so long.'

'I wasn't *that* slow!' complained Tom.

'Why did you just call him *Tom-Tom*?' asked Gareth.

''Cos he's shaped like a drum,' Adam grinned. 'And because of the name on that huge case of his – Thomas Tomlinson.'

'That's my dad's case,' Tom explained. 'It's a family tradition, like. The first-born in every generation gets called Thomas.'

'Feel sorry for any girl, then,' laughed Gareth.

'Bit of advice, man,' said Adam. 'Don't go crackin' any stupid jokes with these coaches. They ain't got no sense of humour.'

'Are they blind, too?' cut in Eddie. 'Blackbeard said he never saw that kid who got me into trouble.'

'Nor did anybody else, Wonder Boy.'

'Don't you believe me, either?'

Adam gave a shrug.

'What I'm *wondering*,' Eddie said sourly,

18

'is why you came back here for more, when you knew what things were like?'

It was Gareth who answered. 'Look, we all know why we're here. We want to improve our techniques and get good enough to win medals when we're older.'

'*Gold* medals,' Adam corrected him.

'Well, that's what I meant. Just didn't want to sound big-headed.'

'*Goals win Golds*,' Adam said, repeating the coaching mantra they'd taught him at Easter. 'They drone on about goals all the time.'

'So what's your main goal?' asked Gareth.

'The 2020 Olympics,' Adam said above the noise of the dinner gong. 'That's when I'm gonna grab gold in the long jump and 100 metres!'

Fifty boys sat in the library after the evening meal, listening to a lecture from Blackbeard on the importance of setting short and long-term goals. To Eddie's disappointment, but not to his surprise, there was no sign of the mystery runner.

No questions were allowed and it was only afterwards – when glasses of green juice were served – that the athletes were able to speak to one another.

'Yeuch!' said Gareth as he took a sip. 'This is really foul. It's even worse than the yellow stuff we had with dinner.'

'Did warn you, GG,' Adam chuckled.

'GG?' repeated Gareth. 'You make me sound like a horse.'

'A giraffe,' Adam explained. 'Gareth the giraffe, with them long, thin legs of yours.'

Gareth smiled. 'So what are we going to call Adam, guys?'

'Don't know yet,' said Tom, 'but I'm sure we'll come up with something soon...'

The French coach interrupted the conversation. 'Drink up, *mes garçons*,' he said, seeing their glasses were still almost full. 'Show them, Fox, 'ow much you enjoy it.'

Adam downed his drink in one gulp, trying not to taste it or choke.

'*Bon!*' exclaimed Petit Pierre, moving away with a thin smile on his face.

'Good boy, *Foxy!*' Eddie chuckled, taking care that nobody was looking as he poured the contents of his own glass into a nearby potted plant.

Chapter Three
Is Anybody There?

The French coach pushed the boys to their limits, and even beyond, during the Tuesday-morning fitness session in the gym. Tom was sick again, losing his breakfast this time.

'Too much toast and jam, I theenk,' said Petit Pierre, prodding Tom's bulging waistline. 'We must make all this fat into muscle, *oui?*'

'*Oui* – I mean, yes, Coach.'

The coach showed no mercy. Every time he blew the whistle, the boys had to do another set of exercises, including press-ups, sit-ups and step-ups.

'Count to ten, *en français* – *un, deux, trois…*'

The afternoon session was spent outdoors under grey clouds, with the athletes split into small groups to be coached in their own events. The training camp had wonderful facilities, including a six-lane, 400-metre running track with an all-weather surface.

'Wicked!' exclaimed Gareth at the sight of the high-jump area with its large, blue landing cushions.

'Only the best here, man,' said Adam, who was on his way towards the long-jump pit. 'This is what makes it worth all the torture.'

'Gramps won't believe his eyes when he sees this place now. He came here as a kid when the Old Manor was a boarding school,' Gareth explained. 'He reckons the house is haunted and that it's got secret passages.'

'I'd like to meet your gramps. Is he comin' to the Open Day?'

'You bet! No way he's gonna miss the chance to have a good old nose around.'

As Adam and Gareth went their separate ways, Tom was anxiously waiting to find out who would be coaching the group of throwers. He was relieved to see Petit Pierre start working with a few hurdlers, but his heart sank when the head coach strode towards the discus area.

'Oh, God! Not Blackbeard!'

In the middle of the arena, Eddie was loosening up with the other distance runners under the supervision of a coach that he hadn't seen before, a young man with long, blond-streaked hair. He looked fit enough to outrun all of them.

'I've put cones right round the track, boys,' he said. 'I want you to change gear every time you come to one. Sprint, jog, sprint, jog – OK?'

Pleased to find this coach appearing more friendly, Eddie thought of him as *Blondie*, and felt brave enough to ask a question.

'Are we going to have any proper races while we're here, Coach? I mean, against some other kids?'

'Maybe,' said Blondie, and then he smiled. 'In fact, by the sounds of it, Eddie, I think you might already have met one of them…'

After the evening lecture in the library, Gareth made sure that none of the coaches were looking and then aimed a kick beneath the table he was sharing with his roommates.

'Ow!' Adam complained. 'Watch it, GG! That was my knee.'

'Bang on target,' Gareth chuckled.

'What d'yer want?'

'I want to know what we're going to do now?'

'Dunno,' Adam muttered. 'Any ideas?'

'Well, we *could* make a start on our new training diaries…' Gareth suggested.

'You've *got* to be jokin'.'

'Or we could go on a ghost hunt,' he grinned. 'I'd like to be able to tell Gramps that we've been trying to track down some of his ghosts.'

Tom pulled a face. 'Count me out, if you're going off exploring. I don't fancy pushing my luck with these coaches.'

'You with us, Wonder Boy?' said Adam. 'You never know, we might even come across your mystery runner up in the attic!'

Eddie shrugged. 'OK, Foxy,' he said, not rising to the bait. 'I wouldn't mind having a word with him.'

'See yer later, Tom-Tom,' said Adam, standing up. 'Don't go drinkin' all that juice now. You never know what's in it.'

Left alone at the table, Tom opened his training diary. Right there on the front page was the bold heading in capital letters:

GOALS WIN GOLDS

'Huh!' he grunted and took another swig of fruit juice. 'I know what *my* main goal is here – avoiding Blackbeard and Petit Pierre as much as possible – they're slave-drivers!'

The three explorers climbed the central staircase as far as the second-floor landing.

'So where did Tom say that old guy appeared yesterday?' asked Gareth.

'Think it was on the next floor,' said Eddie.

'Nah, that's where the coaches' rooms are,' Adam told them. 'Must've happened right at the top of the house.'

Like Tom, Eddie didn't much fancy the prospect of tangling with Blackbeard again. 'That must be out of bounds,' he said. 'What will we do if we get caught?'

Adam gave a shrug. 'Just say we got lost.'

'Oh, yeah,' scoffed Eddie. 'They're likely to believe that, aren't they?'

'So what? The coaches don't scare me. But ghosts – now that's different.'

'No such things as ghosts,' Eddie told him.

'What, not even ones that do cross country?' grinned Adam, slipping him a wink. 'Right, up we go. After you, GG.'

'Why me?'

''Cos you're the one who suggested this ghost-huntin' lark, that's why.'

'It's not because you're frightened then, Foxy?'

Adam pushed Gareth forwards, and he tripped over the bottom step. 'That's right, make loads of noise. Warn everyone we're comin'.'

'Who?'

'Well, all them ghosties for a start. We don't want to scare 'em away, do we!'

Gareth led the way cautiously up the next flight of wooden stairs. 'Wish they wouldn't creak so much,' he hissed.

Adam chuckled. 'Watch any ghost film – the stairs always creak.'

'Anybody there?' asked Eddie from behind, as they reached the next landing.

'You make it sound like we're holdin' a séance. *Is anybody there? Knock twice for yes...*'

Adam didn't get any further. The sound of two bangs came from somewhere along the corridor and the boys fled, thumping down the stairs like an avalanche of rocks, and then making a dash for their room.

They threw themselves onto the bunks and waited, hearts in mouths, for any sound of pursuit. When the door began to open, they froze, watching in horror.

Tom walked in. 'Thought you lot were chasing ghosts,' he said, smirking. 'Get cold feet, did you?'

'Rubbish!' snorted Adam.

'There was nothing up there so we came back down,' Gareth lied.

'Might even make a start on our diaries,' said Eddie.

'I don't know what to put in mine,' Tom admitted.

'Just make it up,' said Adam. 'That's what I did at Easter. Write how you beat Wonder Boy in the cross country. Nobody's gonna bother readin' it.'

'Can't take the risk,' Tom said. 'Anyway, I

don't mind coming last. If you go at your own pace, you get more time to admire the view.'

'So what did the snail see that the fox missed?' Adam sneered.

'Well, all those graves on the island for a start.'

'Even *I* saw them,' said Eddie.

'OK, so what about that statue near the lake?' asked Tom. 'Bet none of you had the chance to read the name on its base.'

They all looked at each other blankly.

'Gareth *Taffy* Jones,' Tom said smugly, putting on an accent. 'He's Welsh, see, boyos, just like Blackbeard.'

'Taffy Jones!' exclaimed Gareth, shocked. 'He was a friend of Gramps at school here. I'm named after him.'

'You called Taffy as well, then?' asked Eddie.

'No, I'm not Welsh, despite my surname being Davies,' said Gareth. 'But Taffy won loads of medals in his athletics career. Big star, he was, in his day.'

'Never heard of him,' Adam snorted. 'I'm no good at ancient history.'

'Well, Gramps will tell you all about him.'

'Guess old Taffy might even be buried on that island,' said Eddie. 'I wonder…'

Chapter Four
The Prowler

Wednesday proved a long, tiring day with tough training sessions before and after a light lunch.

'Didn't think we'd have to do so much running,' moaned Gareth during their mid-afternoon break. 'I've hardly done any actual jumping yet.'

He was standing next to Adam at the drinks trolley, where there was a selection of coloured fruit juices and water. They both chose water.

Adam took a swig from a bottle before replying. 'Yeah, they're sure big on fitness here,' he said, wiping a sleeve across his mouth.

'Poor Tom's really suffering, look.' Gareth pointed towards where Tom was slumped against a cart full of equipment. From a distance, his face was about the same colour as the green juice.

Adam patted his flat stomach. 'Tom-Tom's more of an all-rounder than the rest of us,' he smirked. 'He could do with losin' a few kilos.'

'Bet even Eddie will be skinnier by the time we leave. Just look at him go.'

As they watched the end of an 800-metre practice race, Eddie put on a burst of speed along the far side of the track to surge past two runners, then kicked again as he hit the home straight to leave them trailing in his slipstream.

'Don't know how he does it,' said Adam, shaking his head.

'He still got beaten by some kid the other day,' Gareth replied. 'Whoever *he* was.'

'Yeah, maybe,' Adam said with a shrug, tossing the empty bottle into a bin. 'Reckon he only ran part of the course so he was still fresh, like, for a sprint finish.'

'But why would he send Eddie the wrong way?'

'How should *I* know, man? Might even have been part of a plan – y'know, so they could see how Wonder Boy reacted.'

Adam's attention was caught by some movement at a small window right at the top of the house. Somebody had opened the curtain, looked out briefly and then vanished from view, but not before Adam picked out the white hair.

His mind went back to Easter, when an old man with long, straggly, white hair had sometimes been seen wandering along the dormitory corridors. Adam called him *the prowler*, but the joke failed to be funny when Jacko, one of his roommates, was taken away after taunting the man with the nickname.

The last Adam saw of Jacko was early the following morning as he climbed into the back of a Jeep, which then roared off down the drive. Sitting in the front passenger seat next to Blackbeard was the man with white hair.

'Must be the same guy Tom-Tom met on Monday,' Adam muttered to himself as he wandered towards the long-jump pit. 'Got to be.'

Wendsday

I came frist in the 800m this afternoone. Noboddy beet me this time! It was a good race as we all whanted to impres Coach and he sed Id dune well so I felte quit proude of mylesf.

Eddie looked at what he'd written in his training diary and sighed. He knew some of the words would be wrong, but hoped the neatness might make up for it. Then he realised that

Blondie, who was on duty in the library after the evening lecture, was standing behind him.

'Hmm, your spelling's not too hot, is it, Eddie?' he observed.

'Sorry, Coach,' he murmured, turning red.

'You can't be good at everything,' Blondie said with a smile. 'What's your reading like?'

'Not brilliant,' Eddie admitted. He didn't see any point in trying to hide his difficulties, guessing such weaknesses would soon be picked up here.

'Looking at this, I'd say you might even be dyslexic.'

Eddie had heard that word used at school. 'My teacher said she was going to get me tested, but nothing's happened yet.'

'OK, don't worry. I'll make a note of it in your records so that the other coaches know about it, too.'

Eddie decided it might be a good time to seek permission for something that he'd been planning to do as soon as he had the chance.

'Um, Coach,' he began. 'Can I go out by myself some time, for an extra run?'

'Sure, Eddie. So long as you stay within the Camp grounds.'

'Thanks, Coach,' he said, relieved that Blondie had not insisted that somebody else went with him. 'Only I like running on my own, y'know, solo, like...'

'Sure, I know how you feel,' the young coach drawled. 'Just remember to write in your diary afterwards how it went, OK?'

On the other side of the library, Adam scraped back his chair and snapped his diary shut to hide the half-finished entry. 'Goin' up to the room,' he told Gareth. 'I'm well bored doin' this.'

Left on his own, Gareth's gaze wandered over the nearest bookshelves until it fixed on a thick, red volume. 'Hmm... that might be worth a look,' he mused, going across to investigate.

Adam trudged up the stairs to the second floor, but as he turned towards their dormitory he saw a white-haired man shuffle away along the gloomy corridor.

'The prowler!' he breathed.

Adam pressed himself against a door, hoping to avoid detection, but his presence had not gone unnoticed. The old man stopped and stared back at him, his lined face creasing up still further into a mirthless grin. Then he reached out to touch the wall and passed clean through it, out of sight.

Adam felt a chill tingle down the length of his spine. He forced himself to take a few unsteady steps nearer to where the man had disappeared, but there was just a length of wall covered in dingy, dark-patterned paper. He stumbled back down the corridor and almost fell into the dormitory.

Tom was lying on his bed. 'What's wrong with you, Foxy? You look like you've just seen a ghost!'

'Think I might have,' Adam muttered, but he had no chance to explain before Gareth burst through the door, brandishing a book.

'What's that?' asked Tom.

'Close,' Gareth grinned. 'It's *Who's Who*!'

He read them a short entry about the athletics career of Gareth Jones.

'Is Taffy still alive?' asked Adam.

'He was when this was published. There's no date of his death.'

'Well, dead or alive, I reckon I've just seen him.'

'Where?'

'C'mon, I'll show you,' said Adam, hauling Tom off the bed, despite his protests. 'Both of you.'

He led them up the corridor and stopped near the fire escape. 'This is where Taffy disappeared,' he said, tapping on the wall.

'How do you know it was him?' demanded Tom.

'Who else could it be?'

'Anybody!'

Adam ignored him. 'Thought it was a ghost at first, but that's stupid. And he looked solid enough, even if this wall isn't. Listen!' He tapped again. 'Sounds hollow to me. You try it, GG.'

'Look, I don't know if this is really a good idea,' said Gareth.

'Well, it *was* yours in the first place,' Adam reminded him. 'You said you wanted to brag to your gramps that you'd done some ghostbustin'. So now's your chance. This must be one of them secret passages he told you about.'

Gareth sighed and began to press on the wall with both hands, checking for any tell-tale sign of movement. 'This is crazy,' he muttered. 'We're just wasting our…' As Gareth leant his weight against the wall, it suddenly slid open and swallowed him up like a hungry mouth.

Adam gawped at the black hole and only just managed to jam his leg against the wall as it tried to close the gap. 'GG?' he hissed. 'You OK?'

'Think so,' came the reply as Gareth regained his feet, rubbing his shoulder. 'Just fell a bit heavily.'

'You high jumpers are too used to havin' a cushioned landing,' Adam chuckled. 'Looks a bit dark in there. Go and get us a torch, Tom-Tom.'

As Tom gladly left them to it, Adam shifted his position to ease the strain on his leg and the wall rumbled further across, almost trapping him.

'Let me get out!' yelled Gareth.

'Can't – there's no room.' Adam wriggled the rest of his body through the narrow space and the wall shut tight behind him.

'Oh, that's just great!' Gareth said sarcastically. 'Well done, Foxy!'

It took a while for their eyes to become accustomed to the gloom, but at least there was a faint light coming from somewhere above.

'Looks like the only way is up,' said Adam.

'What about Tom?'

'He's no use. C'mon, let's check it out.'

Half a dozen stone steps led up onto a small landing and the light improved as the boys turned a corner and reached the bottom of a metal, spiral staircase.

'Probably goes right up to the attic,' Gareth said. 'Servants' quarters once, I bet.'

Holding onto the hand rail, they tiptoed up the winding steps and found themselves in a short corridor. The first door was locked but when Adam tested the next, the handle turned and it swung open. They were relieved to find the small room unoccupied.

'Not exactly the five-star suite, is it?' Adam muttered, wrinkling his nose as they went inside. 'Smells like something's died in here – but not recently.'

Their attention was caught by a display of faded black-and-white photographs on a wall opposite the single bed. They were mostly snaps of a young athlete in action – running, jumping and throwing – but one of them showed him holding up a medal and giving the camera a wide, toothy grin.

'Must be Taffy, yonks ago,' Adam said. 'Just look at that baggy kit.'

'Can't wait to tell Gramps about this,' Gareth chuckled. 'Bet he'll want to sneak up here himself when he…'

Gareth froze in mid-sentence. The bare floorboards behind them had creaked and neither he nor Adam dared to look round.

'Lost, are you, boyos?' warbled a voice in a lilting, Welsh accent. 'Long time since Old Taffy's had any visitors up here…'

Chapter Five
Boat Trip

'Where's *he* off to in such a hurry?' said Tom, seeing Eddie nip out of the library straight after Thursday's evening lecture. 'He hasn't done his diary yet.'

'That kid's always in a hurry, man,' said Adam. 'Except when he's writin' of course. He takes yonks over doin' that.'

'He's gone out for an extra run,' Gareth told them.

'What!' gasped Tom. 'He must be a sucker for punishment. What is it with you people?'

'How d'yer mean?' Adam muttered, leaning back in his chair.

'Well, you seem to go looking for trouble. I really thought you two were for the high jump after you got nabbed last night.'

'That's GG's event, not mine,' Adam said with a grin. 'But you should've seen Blackbeard's face when he found us with Taffy! He was dead mad.'

Tom shook his head. 'I still can't believe that Taffy's his father.'

'Well, it's true. The old man told us himself,' Gareth assured him. 'That's why Blackbeard couldn't do anything. And he won't dare touch us now we're in Taffy's good books.'

'Just don't push your luck,' Tom warned. 'I wouldn't trust either further than I could throw 'em – which ain't very far.'

'Taffy seems harmless enough,' said Gareth. 'He was so pleased when I explained I was named after him because of Gramps. I think they were sort of partners-in-crime here as schoolmates – always sneaking off together and getting into scrapes.'

'Exactly,' Tom muttered.

'Reckon that's why old Taffy let on about the secret tunnel under his statue,' put in Adam, ignoring Tom's interruption. 'Y'know, boastin' like, so we'd tell your gramps about it, too.'

'Hope that's not where Eddie's gone now,' said Gareth, suddenly worried. 'He wouldn't go down there to explore it by himself, would he?'

'Nah! Even Wonder Boy's not that daft,' Adam scoffed, but then had second thoughts. 'Is he...?'

By the time the trio got back to their dormitory, Eddie had changed into his kit and was already running through the trees towards the statue by the lake.

'Wonder if Taffy was telling the truth about the tunnel,' he mused.

A few minutes later, he halted in front of the statue to have a closer look. It showed the muscular figure in his prime, medals draped around his neck, posing with a discus clutched in one huge hand and a javelin held aloft in the other.

Carved into the base in capital letters was the athlete's name and proud title.

GARETH 'TAFFY' JONES
OLYMPIC CHAMPION

'Can't be bad, having that on your statue,' Eddie murmured, impressed.

He was tempted to test out what Taffy had said about the statue, but he had another aim in mind tonight. He stared across the water at the island and then continued his run along the edge of the lake past the chapel until he arrived at the derelict boathouse.

To Eddie's relief, its only occupant, a rowing boat, appeared to be in reasonable condition. He dragged it into the water and clambered in. The fact that it was still floating ten metres from the bank boosted his confidence.

'Not sunk yet, anyway,' he grunted, pulling awkwardly on the single oar.

The boat turned in a clumsy circle before he managed to control it better and he soon bumped into the island.

Eddie scrambled out, getting his shoes full of water in the process, and heaved the boat up onto the grassy bank. Although the island was well screened from the Old Manor, he made sure he kept out of sight in the shelter of the trees. He bent to examine the group of seven white crosses more closely and saw that each had a small brass plate with an engraved code number, starting with T1. 'Wonder why they don't have names?' he murmured.

After learning that Taffy was still alive, Eddie had thought that this might be a pet cemetery, but now he ruled out that, too. One thing he did discover, however, was that there was a missing number in the sequence. There was no T3.

His curiosity now satisfied, Eddie decided to head back before he was found out. The return trip was not without mishap and he breathed a sigh of relief when he finally got out of the wobbly boat.

'Pity I lost that,' he murmured, staring at the oar, which was now tangled in a clump of reeds out of reach.

Eddie turned and jogged back towards the house to the accompaniment of his squelching shoes, but his absence had not gone unnoticed.

'Been paddling, have you, laddie?'

Eddie had been jogging across the courtyard when Blackbeard stepped out from the dark archway of the main entrance. He stopped in his tracks and his heart sank at the prospect of another ducking in the pool.

'Er… I've just been out for a run, Coach,' he began. 'I got permission from…'

Blackbeard cut him short. 'So I've heard, Peters. And I've also been told you could be dyslexic.'

'Yes, sorry, Coach, I can't help it, like…'

'Not your fault, laddie,' Blackbeard said before making a startling admission. 'So is Taffy Jones.'

After a hot shower, Eddie found his roommates in the games room and he had to explain what he'd been up to in rather more detail. He also told them about his encounter with Blackbeard.

'You were taking a huge risk,' said Tom, who had a glass of green juice in his hand as he watched the others playing table football.

'Not really. Blondie said I could go.'

'Yes, go running, not messing about in a boat.'

'Just wanted to check things out, that's all,' Eddie said with a shrug. 'Wonder what the letter T on the crosses stands for?'

'T for Taffy?' Gareth suggested. 'But then why isn't there a T3, like you said?'

'C'mon, are you playin' or not, GG?' Adam said impatiently.

'I'm listening to Eddie.'

'Huh! Just 'cos you're losin'.'

'No, I'm not.'

'Yes, you are. It's 3–2 to me.'

'Wonder if Taffy actually owns this place,' Eddie said, cutting across their argument.

Adam sighed. 'Here we go, another theory from Wonder Boy. First you have him dead and buried, and now you've got him down as the big boss man.'

'Well, what do *you* think, Mr Know-It-All?'

As Gareth sent the next ball onto the table, Adam twisted his handle grip sharply and one of the footballers spun and smacked the metal ball into the goal with a loud clunk.

'4-2!' he cried.

'Offside!' claimed Gareth.

'Rubbish!' Adam scoffed. 'There's no such thing as offside in this.'

'It still doesn't count. I wasn't ready.'

'So what *do* you think, Foxy?' said Tom. 'C'mon, let's have your great theory.'

'Ain't got one,' Adam admitted, 'but if you must know, Old Taffy gives me the creeps, the way he prowls about the place. And 'cos I know he was lyin' last night when I asked him about Jacko. Y'know, that kid I palled up with at Easter – the one I told you got took away.'

'What did Taffy say?' asked Eddie.

'He reckoned he knew nothin' about him – but I saw 'em together in the Jeep.'

'Where do you think they were going?' put in Gareth.

'No idea,' Adam grunted. 'But I bet it wasn't a ride home.'

Chapter Six
The Statue

'Thought this was meant to be a *summer* camp!' moaned Gareth, resting on his bunk after Friday's fitness sessions. 'It's hardly stopped raining since we got here.'

Due to the bad weather, the boys had endured an extra workout in the gym under the demanding eye and sharp tongue of Petit Pierre. Even when the sun did break through for a short time, it was a frustrating experience for most of the athletes. Runners and jumpers were hampered by the wet conditions, while the throwers had to keep drying the equipment to help their grip on the javelin, shot and discus.

'Blondie said the forecast is better for the weekend,' Eddie told his roommates. 'At least it should be fine for the Open Day.'

'So what about tomorrow, then, guys?' said Adam. 'That's our best chance.'

'For what?' said Tom, coming into the room.

'I'm talkin' about the statue,' said Adam. 'Y'know, checkin' it out, like.'

'Sounds a bit dodgy, if you ask me,' said Tom, pulling a face.

'Nobody's askin' you,' Adam replied and turned back to the others. 'Look, we've got trainin' in the mornin', then we're free. The coaches have Sat'day afternoon off.'

'Bet Blackbeard stays here,' Eddie muttered. 'He's never off duty.'

'Even so,' Adam went on, 'I reckon we can still sneak away.'

'I suppose so,' said Gareth. 'But after all this rain, we could be up to our necks in water down that tunnel.'

'*If* it exists,' Eddie added.

'At least it's worth a look, eh?' said Adam. 'What d'yer say, guys?'

'OK,' agreed Gareth, reluctantly.

'Sure,' Eddie said with a shrug.

'You must be mad,' muttered Tom. 'C'mon, let's get to that dining room. It's fish and chips tonight and I'm starving.'

The clock on the tallest tower of the Old Manor struck twice on the Saturday afternoon as the four boys stood in front of the larger-than-life statue of the young Taffy Jones.

'Don't look much like he does now,' muttered Adam.

'I bet Gramps will still recognise him if he shows up tomorrow,' said Gareth.

'Wonder what they'll say to each other after all those years,' said Eddie.

Tom checked back nervously towards the house, glad that trees were shielding the statue from view. He still didn't really know why he had agreed to join in, apart from not wanting to be left out. 'Just hope nobody has followed us,' he murmured.

'Quit witterin', will yer, Tom–Tom,' Adam snapped. 'Let's do it.'

Taffy had told them how to gain entrance to the tunnel but Adam did not really expect anything to happen. He stamped on the stone discus at the base of the statue, tilting it at an angle. Then, with the grating noise of a rusty mechanism, the front of the plinth began to slide slowly forward.

'Open, sez me!' Adam whooped in triumph.

'It's not very big,' said Tom, peering at the black hole beneath the statue.

'Big enough for a secret passage,' replied Adam, shining a torch down it. 'Reckon even you can squeeze in there, if you hold your belly in a bit.' He led the way, dropping to the ground and squirming backwards into the hole until he stubbed his toes against something solid. 'Ladder!' he cried. 'Just like Taffy said.'

A dim light suddenly shone from the hole.

'Good, Foxy's found the switch as well,' said Gareth. 'Taffy told us the tunnel was discovered when his statue was put up. He thinks it must've been dug out centuries ago, but he had it all wired up with electric light.'

One by one, they copied Adam's entry technique and joined him in a small chamber before shuffling off, half-crouched, down a low, narrow channel with damp walls and a wet, sloping floor.

'We must be going right under the lake,' breathed Eddie.

'Good job it hasn't flooded,' hissed Tom. 'I can't swim, remember.'

'If the roof gets any lower, I'll be doing the

49

crawl,' panted Gareth, who was already bent double.

Fortunately for all of them, the tunnel became a little higher and also drier as it began to climb upwards, before coming to an abrupt halt.

'Dead end?' said Eddie, staring at the wall in front of them. 'It's been bricked up.'

'Must be a way out somehow,' said Adam. 'Start lookin', gang.'

They probed the tunnel walls until Tom found a small lever tucked into a recess in the rock. As he gave it a tug, two things happened. First, all the lights went out and the boys were plunged into blackness – then a welcome shaft of daylight appeared as a section of the brick wall began to creak open. The relieved group scrambled through the gap and along a short tunnel, which emerged in a wood.

'Looks like an old mineshaft,' observed Gareth, glancing back at the overgrown exit. 'It's well camouflaged. You'd be lucky to find it again amongst all these trees.'

'Belt up, GG!' said Adam. 'I can hear voices.'

They all listened.

'Coming from over there,' Gareth said, pointing to the right. 'Let's go and see.'

'Think we should?' Eddie whispered. 'I mean, we don't want to get done.'

'*Done*?' Adam repeated. 'Who's gonna *do* us, Wonder Boy?'

Eddie shrugged. 'Well, we could be trespassing on private property.'

Adam ignored him. 'Just break off some branches as we go through the wood so we can follow the trail back here,' he ordered before striding away.

It wasn't long before their progress was halted again – this time by a high, mesh fence with lengths of barbed wire stretched along the top.

'Guess they don't want anybody to get in,' said Gareth.

'Or out,' muttered Adam.

The boys followed the line of the fence as best they could, though they were hampered by the undergrowth, which was full of nettles.

'Look!' cried Eddie when they gained their first clear view. 'Another track!'

They stared through the fence at an athletics track, where a group of young runners were training.

'You sure we haven't somehow stumbled back to B.A.S.E. Camp?' said Tom.

'Positive. Our track has six lanes,' Eddie told him. 'This one's only got four.'

'So who are *these* guys?' Adam demanded.

In response, Eddie let out a gasp of surprise. 'Well, for a start, there's that kid who got me into all that trouble.'

'Which one is he?' asked Tom.

'The one out in front, of course.'

'Thought you didn't get a good look at him,' Adam sneered.

'Not his face, but I'd know that running style anywhere. That's definitely him.'

Adam had recognised somebody, too. 'And I know the one who's behind him!' he said, nodding.

'Who is it?' asked Gareth.

'Jacko.'

'What's *he* doing here?'

'Dunno,' Adam muttered, 'but I sure intend to find out.'

Chapter Seven
A.C.E.

The four boys kept out of sight among the trees as they watched the runners finish their training and flop down for a brief rest not far from the fence. The presence of a coach, however, made an attempt at contact too risky.

Led by Adam, they crept along the fringe of the wood instead, until they came to a single-track road and padlocked gates.

'There's a notice on the gates,' said Eddie.

'Advanced Centre of Excellence,' Tom read out. 'Huh! The initials spell A.C.E.'

'Sure puts us in our place at B.A.S.E. Camp, eh?' Gareth muttered. 'These kids here must be a cut above.'

'They'll have to prove it first,' said Adam.

'I think one of them already has,' Tom said, winking at Eddie.

Before Eddie could respond, Adam came to a decision. 'C'mon, gang, let's go back,' he urged.

'Gotta speak to Jacko somehow. He'll tell us what's goin' on here.'

That was easier said than done. The A.C.E. athletes were now doing stretching exercises further away from the fence, so Adam began jumping up and down, waving his arms, to attract Jacko's attention.

It wasn't only Jacko who noticed him. Adam's antics were spotted by a number of the athletes, making them point and laugh. The coach turned to detect the source of the distraction, but Adam had already dived for cover in the undergrowth.

'Did he see you?' Tom demanded from his hiding place behind a tree.

'Jacko? Yeah, think so.'

'I meant the coach.'

Gareth peeped through the bushes. 'It's OK. He's making them do press-ups now. Punishment for laughing, I bet.'

'Don't this lot have any free time?' said Eddie. 'I mean, it *is* Saturday afternoon.'

'Probably lucky if they even get time to eat,' Adam said with a smirk. 'Pity poor old Tom-Tom if *he* got sent here!'

After about ten more minutes of exercises,

the coach ended the session and the group broke up. Most of the athletes wandered off, but two of them began to play with a tennis ball, tossing it back and forth as they jogged around the track.

'Jacko's headin' this way,' Adam grinned. 'Knew he would.'

'And look who's coming with him,' Eddie muttered.

Jacko deliberately let the ball go past him and then kicked it into the long grass near the fence so that they would have to go and search for it.

'Watcha, Jacko!' Adam greeted him.

'Thought it was you, Foxy, dancing about like a nutcase.'

'What the hell are you doin' here?'

'I've been here since Easter. Thought they were going to throw me out for calling that old man "the prowler", but they brought me here instead. I've been doing loads of running,' he said, and then nodded towards Eddie. 'Just like your new mate, I gather.'

Eddie hadn't taken his eyes off the other lad, who had now found the ball.

'Hey! Wonder Boy!' said Adam. 'Bet you can't beat Jacko over 400 metres.'

'Maybe not,' Eddie replied sourly, 'but I'd like to have another race against his pal.'

The black-haired boy chuckled, flipping the ball casually from hand to hand as they all stared at him.

'We met before, man?' said Adam. 'You look kinda familiar.'

The boy spoke for the first time. 'You most likely heard my name,' he said in a lilting voice.

'And what's that?'

'Taffy Jones,' he replied, enjoying their surprised reaction. 'But everybody calls me YT.'

'YT?' repeated Tom.

'Yeah – Young Taffy!' he giggled.

Gareth was the first to respond. 'So are you Old Taffy's grandson or something?'

'Or something…'

Eddie wasn't satisfied with that answer. 'And what does that mean exactly?'

Young Taffy grinned. 'Don't know if you lot are ready for the *exact* bit yet. What do you think, Jacko?'

Jacko shrugged. 'Might as well tell 'em, YT.'

'Yeah, why not?' he agreed. 'Don't suppose they'll believe me, anyway.'

'Try us,' grunted Tom.

'OK, then,' he said. 'I'm not his grandson – or even his son. I *am* Taffy Jones…'

Adam butted in. 'You've already told us yer name.'

'You're not listening to what I'm saying,' he replied calmly. 'I'm *him* and he's *me*.'

'That don't make no sense, man.'

'It does if you're a clone!'

Beeeeeeeppp!

The intruders had no chance to recover from their shock at such a revelation, nor ask any further questions. The long blast on the coach's whistle was quickly followed by two more.

'You've been spotted,' cried Jacko. 'Leg it – fast!'

As the others turned to go, Adam hesitated. 'You ain't seen the last of us, Taffy Boy,' he promised. 'We'll be back.'

Young Taffy shrugged. 'Not if the dogs get you first,' he said with a sly grin.

Loud barking could now be heard from the far side of the track.

'Beat it, Foxy!' urged Jacko. 'Those brutes don't ask questions.'

'A *fox* hunt!' cackled Young Taffy. 'Tally-ho!'

Adam shot him a dirty look, nodded to Jacko and was gone, lost to sight among the trees. He soon caught up with the rest. Their panicky flight had taken them into the wood on a different course from before and they had halted in a small clearing, trying to get their bearings.

'Which way now?' gasped Tom, red-faced.

'Not sure,' Gareth confessed.

'We could try and skirt back round the lake,' suggested Eddie.

'What, with them great mutts on the loose behind us!' exclaimed Adam.

'He's right,' said Gareth. 'The tunnel's safer. It can't be far away.'

'Just find it, will you,' Tom demanded. 'I don't want to end up as dog meat.'

It was more by luck than judgement that the group stumbled upon the same path they had used when leaving the tunnel.

'We're OK!' whooped Eddie in relief, pointing to some broken branches. 'Here's the trail Foxy got me to make.'

'Good job you did what you were told for once,' Adam grinned. 'Well done, Wonder Boy!'

They soon found the concealed entrance and disappeared inside the narrow tunnel that led to the brick wall. They scrambled through the gap and waited until Tom found the lever to re-close the wall and switch the light circuit back on.

'Phew!' breathed Gareth. 'That was close. Can't hear the dogs at all now.'

'C'mon, let's get back,' urged Tom. 'I'm hungry.'

'Huh!' grunted Adam. 'Don't worry if you hear any rumblin' noises, guys. It's not the roof cavin' in — just Tom-Tom's belly playin' up!'

In single file, the boys made their way through the tunnel under the lake until they reached the ladder. Gareth clambered up it first and peered through the gap beneath the statue.

'All clear,' he announced. 'We're in luck.'

It was only after they had all got out of the hole that a dark figure emerged from the nearby trees. He was not alone. Straining forward on a tight leash was a big, black dog.

'Reckon our luck's just run out,' muttered Adam.

'Welcome back to B.A.S.E.,' Blackbeard said grimly. 'Don't forget to close that hole. Somebody might get hurt…'

The boys were confined to their room for the rest of the day after being lectured by Blackbeard for straying off limits. The head coach also made them promise not to say anything to their families during the Open Day about what had happened.

In exchange for their silence, they would be allowed to stay at B.A.S.E. Camp and complete the coaching course. It was an uneasy – and temporary – truce.

'Thought human clonin' wasn't possible,' said Adam, sprawled on his bunk.

'Yes, it's possible, all right,' Gareth replied. 'Just not done, that's all.'

'Why not?'

Gareth shrugged. 'Not sure. Might even be illegal, for all I know.'

Tom picked at the remains of the meat-paste sandwiches, which had been sent up to the dormitory as their meal, along with glasses of juice. He was still hungry.

'Scientists have done it with animals,' Tom told them, 'but it's supposed to be very difficult with humans.'

'Well, they seem to have managed it here somehow,' reasoned Gareth. 'YT's the proof of that.'

'Strange he didn't mind admitting it,' said Tom. 'Even boasted about it, really.'

'Old Taffy likes to show off, too,' Adam muttered. 'Maybe they *are* one and the same, sort of thing.'

'You're very quiet, Eddie,' said Gareth. 'What do *you* think about all this business?'

'I think it stinks even worse than Foxy's feet!' he said, pulling a face. 'YT's a freak!'

Chapter Eight
Open Day

'There you are, Gramps!' Gareth exclaimed. 'What do you think of that?'

Gramps stared, open-mouthed, at the statue of his old schoolfriend. 'Taffy Jones…' he breathed. 'I can hardly believe it.'

'We said you'd be in for a big surprise,' laughed Gareth. He exchanged grins with Adam, who had managed to slip away from his parents for a while to meet Gramps and show him what they had discovered.

Adam glanced towards the house to make sure no one was watching and then stamped on the stone discus. 'Watch this!' he cried.

Gareth enjoyed Gramps' shocked reaction as the gap slowly appeared at the base of the statue.

'It's a secret passage,' Gareth told him. 'Just like in your stories about the school.'

'Better than any of them, m'boy,' said Gramps. 'How on earth did you find it?'

'*He* told us.'

'Who?'

'Taffy!'

'You mean the old boy's still here?' Gramps gasped. 'You've actually met him?'

'Sure have,' said Gareth. 'He might even own the place, for all we know.'

Gramps shook his head, marvelling at such news. 'Taffy Jones!' he repeated in amazement. 'Thought he were dead.'

Adam laughed. 'So did we at first. Thought he might have been one of your ghosts when I saw him disappear through a wall.'

'Through a wall?'

'Yeah – turned out to be another secret passage.'

'The old devil!' Gramps murmured. 'Don't like to say this now, but you couldn't really trust Taffy as a kid. You never knew if he were just telling tales.'

'Don't reckon he's changed much, then,' muttered Adam, thinking of Taffy's denial over Jacko. 'Only I call it lyin'.'

'Best close this up before anyone comes,' Gareth said, heaving the discus back into position to seal the hole once more.

'Do you know where it leads?' asked Gramps.

'Sure do. A group of us explored it,' said Gareth. 'Goes right under the lake.'

'Goodness!'

Before Gareth could say any more, he saw his mother heading their way across the lawn, carrying a bowl of strawberries.

'I might have known you two would try to escape the crowds,' she chuckled. 'Come on, Gareth, introduce me to your new friend.'

'This is Adam, Mum,' he said and then pointed up at the statue. 'We were just showing Gramps an old one – Gareth Taffy Jones, the great Olympic champion!'

Mum choked and dropped a strawberry off the spoon down the front of her new dress.

Tom and Eddie were finding it less easy to entertain their families. After a guided tour of the Camp's training facilities, there weren't exactly a lot of things to see and do – at least before the demonstration of some track and field events.

Tom was sitting with his parents at one of the tables in the courtyard, conveniently near to where the strawberries were being served.

Two empty bowls bore witness to his appetite and he was planning to go back for a third. He let out a loud burp.

'Manners, Thomas!' said his mother, frowning at him and hoping that none of the nearby guests had heard the noise.

'Sorry, Mum,' he said automatically. 'Do you want any more strawbs?'

Eddie was leading his parents from the running track when his father halted by the pool. 'Been for a swim yet, son?' he asked.

Eddie pulled a face, recalling his humiliation by Blackbeard. 'Just once, Dad,' he replied, moving him on quickly. 'Water's too cold.'

Eddie soon joined Tom in the queue for strawberries and cream. 'Wonder why Blackbeard told everyone about the A.C.E. place?' he said, referring to the speech of welcome, when the head coach announced that some boys might be invited to be coached at an advanced training centre. 'Thought it was supposed to be a big secret.'

Tom burped again. 'Not any more,' he grinned. 'Not since us lot stumbled on it. Probably worried we might go and spill the beans.'

'Huh! Bet all the kids strutting their stuff on the track later will be from there,' Eddie muttered. 'And I hope YT's among them.'

'Why?'

'Oh, nothing,' he said with a shrug. 'Just like to see him in action again, that's all.'

'Hello, Davy!'

Gramps whirled round. Nobody had called him by that name for years.

'It *is* Davy, isn't it? Must be.'

Gramps stared at the old man with long, white hair. He had joined the Davies family on a grassy bank overlooking the running track, where sprint races were in progress. It was only the Welsh accent that gave away his identity.

'Taffy?'

'The one and only,' he replied, and then chuckled. 'Well, maybe that's not quite true no more.'

Gramps failed to appreciate the significance of the remark, and reached out to shake the offered hand. 'Never thought that one day they'd be building statues of rogues like you,' he said, grinning at his old school mate.

'Oh, you've seen that thing, have you? Mind you, I had to pay somebody a small fortune to do it, didn't I?'

'And pay them to keep quiet about the tunnel underneath, no doubt.'

'Young Gareth's shown you that as well, has he?' Taffy replied, slipping the boy a wink. 'Thought he might.'

'You got any grandkids, Taffy?' Gramps asked him.

'No, but there *is* someone who takes after me in a way,' Taffy said and then grinned. 'Chip off the old block, you might say, Davy. See if you can spot him in this next race.'

Gareth knew what *that* must mean. When the bang of a gun signalled the start of the 800-metre event, he went to stand next to Adam and they were not surprised to see who burst into an early lead.

'YT's settin' a real hot pace,' said Adam. 'Even Jacko can't keep up with him.'

'Perhaps he's gone off too fast,' Gareth suggested.

'Nah, reckon he knows what he's doin'. None of 'em will catch him now.'

Gramps was not even aware of the other boys in the race. His mind had lurched back half a century and he could clearly see another young lad, in white, baggy shorts and vest, with the same upright running action.

Taffy Jones was more interested in watching Gramps' reaction. 'Remember when my hair was jet black like that, Davy?' he said.

Gramps nodded, not looking away from the track. 'Aye, and I remember how you ran, too. It's uncanny. Almost identical style.'

'It *is* identical,' Taffy confirmed. 'Coached him myself.'

Young Taffy ran past them to complete the first lap, well in the lead. Then suddenly he found another runner hard on his heels.

'Wonder Boy!' gasped Adam. 'Has he gone mad?'

Eddie had been unable to resist the temptation to dash onto the track and chase after the leader, intent on revenge. Taken by surprise, Young Taffy slowed to glance back and check out his unexpected challenger. It gave Eddie the chance to close the gap and they

68

rounded the bend shoulder to shoulder.

'Now let's see how you like it!' cried Eddie.

The two boys pounded along the back straight, cheered on by the spectators, who assumed it was all part of the entertainment.

'That idiot's really askin' for it!' Adam muttered. 'Blackbeard will go berserk later, when his folks have gone home.'

'Don't suppose Eddie even thought about that,' said Gareth. 'He just wants to get his own back.'

'He might do as well – YT's already run one lap.'

With about 200 metres to go, Eddie accelerated into the bend, hoping his fresher legs would drive him into the clear. He was running as fast as he could, hampered slightly by his tracksuit, but he wasn't able to shake off his rival. Young Taffy was still only just behind him as they entered the home straight.

'He's gonna do it!' screamed Gareth, dancing up and down.

Adam wasn't so sure. 'I wouldn't bet on it…' he began and then gasped in astonishment as Young Taffy suddenly seemed to find an extra gear to surge ahead, making it almost look as if Eddie were going backwards.

As the winner sprinted over the finishing line, arms aloft in triumph, Eddie sagged to his knees, crushed with disappointment.

Adam and Gareth ran across the track to pull him back onto his feet and lead him away.

'What got into you?' Adam demanded. 'That was a crazy thing to do!'

'More like what they've got into *him*!' Eddie stormed. 'You saw what he just did. That's not normal. He must be on drugs!'

'Cool it, Wonder Boy!' Adam warned. 'Here come your folks. Don't go rantin' on to them about drugs and stuff. They'll take you home.'

Gareth and Adam moved off as Eddie's family made a fuss of him.

'What do you think he'll tell them?' said Gareth.

'Not much,' Adam grunted. 'Not if he's got any sense, he won't.'

'Well I'm going to tell Gramps about what's going on here. We need somebody on our side – y'know, just in case.'

'In case of what?'

'I don't know,' Gareth said with a shrug. 'That's what bothers me.'

Chapter Nine
Out of Bounds

'Hi, Foxy!' cried Jacko, as the three boys emerged from the trees. 'Wasn't sure if you'd be able to make it.'

Adam had snatched a word with Jacko after the race and arranged to meet up at the old boathouse during their free Sunday evening, after all the families had left. Gareth and Eddie had come with him.

'You know me, man,' Adam laughed. 'But how did *you* get here?'

'A chain is only as strong as its weakest link,' Jacko said with a sly wink.

'What's that supposed to mean?' asked Gareth.

'It means there's a small hole in the fence.'

'You on your own?' demanded Eddie. 'Or is that freak with you?'

Jacko's grin faded. 'If you mean YT, he's at the Centre, celebrating his victory.'

'Wonder Boy here reckons YT must be takin' drugs, the way he stormed through to win like he did,' Adam said.

Jacko gave a casual shrug. 'We've all had a little extra help.'

'What do you mean by that?' asked Gareth.

'Artificial help,' Jacko admitted. 'Just like you lot.'

'We're not taking anything,' Eddie denied hotly.

'Oh, yes, you are,' Jacko told him. 'It's not just fruit in all that juice they make you drink. It contains special vitamins, too. Y'know, stimulants, like.'

Eddie was not surprised by that revelation. 'I wondered why they keep trying to force it down us. Tastes awful. I pour it away, if I can.'

'Tom-Tom can't get enough of it,' Adam said. 'He's hooked on the stuff.'

'Well, it *is* meant to be addictive. Where is your fat friend, anyway?'

'Probably goin' round the tables, helpin' himself to any leftovers,' Adam chuckled.

Gareth kept on with the questioning. 'It can't be just the juice, though,' he said. 'What other kind of *help* do you lot have at the Centre?'

Jacko didn't see the need to hide anything. 'They gave me an injection at Easter,' he said. 'It's supposed to help muscle growth and increase power. Seems to work, anyway. I'm loads fitter and faster than I used to be.'

'Doesn't it wear off after a while?'

'Don't think so – not for years. The muscles just keep on getting stronger.'

Eddie nodded, satisfied that his suspicions about Young Taffy had been confirmed. 'Explains how YT could run so quickly after 800 metres.'

Jacko grinned. 'Well, he *is* something of a special case of course. Y'know, with him being a clone, like.'

'Yeah, I still don't really get that business,' said Adam. 'Is that kid just another version of Taffy Jones?'

'Not *just* another version. T3 is a sort of souped-up version – a de-luxe model, if you like. He's not even dyslexic.'

Eddie was startled by that fact, as much as by the use of the T3 code name for Young Taffy.

'There's no cross for T3 on the island,' he said, staring at Jacko. 'Are the others for Taffy's clones that didn't survive?'

Jacko shrugged but made no effort to deny it.

'I once read a science-fiction story about this kind of thing,' said Gareth. 'Scientists messed around with a cloned baby's genes and created a monster.'

'Well, it's science *fact* now. It's called genetic engineering,' Jacko told them. 'YT isn't a monster, but he sure is superhuman!'

Munday

Felte good to be back in traning today. I do'nt know how far we ran but even I was a bit tried by the end. Coach told us we'll be haveing midweek races agenst some kids from a club in towne. Hope thay give us some good...

Eddie was going to use the word competition but realised that he had no idea how to spell it. He decided to write contests instead.

...kontestes.

He put down his pen and closed his training diary with relief. He always found writing more tiring than running. He was also relieved – and surprised – that his gatecrashing of the race seemed to have gone unpunished. His humiliation on the track still rankled, but at least he had run some of that disappointment out of his system today.

Adam had not yet started his daily diary and his glass of juice remained untouched. He was still brooding over what Jacko had told them about Young Taffy – and the long-lasting effects of the injection to improve physical performance.

'Can't be *that* bad for you,' he mused, doodling on a piece of paper. 'I mean, Jacko seems OK…'

'Fancy yourself as a bit of an artist, do you?'

Adam jolted upright and realised that Blondie was peering over his shoulder at the design of an interwoven letter and number on the paper.

'Sorry, Coach,' he mumbled. 'Er… just thinkin' what to put, like…'

'Looks like a T and a 3,' Blondie said, raising his eyebrows. 'What do they stand for?'

Adam gave a shrug. 'Don't really know, Coach. Just doodlin'…'

'Right, well I suggest we get rid of that, Fox,' he said, tearing the paper into shreds. 'We don't want other people wondering what they might mean, do we?'

'No, Coach,' Adam agreed reluctantly.

Gareth had been watching this little drama from across the table. 'Guess he didn't think much of your artwork, Foxy,' he grinned when Blondie had taken Eddie to one side of the library to go over his spelling mistakes.

Adam pulled a face. 'How *you* gettin' on?'

'A bit better than you, but not much. Can't write about what I'd really like to.'

Gareth's main problem was how to keep Gramps' mobile out of sight of the coaches. Phones were banned at B.A.S.E. Camp and confiscated upon arrival, but after Gareth explained what had been happening, Gramps had given him his own one.

'I won't be far away, m'boy,' he promised. 'I'll nip home and pick up some things, then come back and find a local hotel. I'll borrow your mother's phone, so you can call me.'

Gareth wasn't sure what Gramps might be able to do, but it was reassuring to know that someone would be close at hand.

'Hi, Gramps! It's me.'

'About time, too, m'boy.'

He sounded cross and Gareth held the phone

further away from his ear.

'You *do* realise it's Tuesday evening,' Gramps complained. 'I've been hanging about this hotel for two days, waiting to hear from you.'

'Sorry, Gramps, but this is the first chance I've had to get away. They've had us working flat out.'

'Is everything all right? You're not in trouble?'

'No – only with the coach for not jumping high enough,' Gareth said with a sigh.

'So where are you now?'

'At the statue. Just me and Foxy. We wanted to see if the tunnel's still OK to use.'

While Gareth was speaking, Adam had opened the entrance and the lower half of his body disappeared into the gap.

'Hey! Wait for me!' Gareth cried.

'What's going on?' came the demand in his ear.

'Hold on a minute, Gramps. I've just got to sort Foxy out.'

He was too late. Adam was already out of reach.

'Doesn't need two of us,' came a voice from the darkness. 'You keep watch.'

Gareth sighed in frustration and spoke into the phone again. 'Sorry, Gramps. I thought we

77

were both going down into the tunnel, but Foxy's gone by himself.'

As Gramps began to say something else, Adam unexpectedly reappeared, scrambling out onto the grass with a squelch.

'What's up?' asked Gareth.

'The water – that's what's up!' Adam grunted, pointing at his soaking jeans. 'They've flooded the tunnel and fused the lights. It's too dark to see where you're goin'.'

'Serves you right,' Gareth chuckled. 'That's the trouble with you long jumpers. You always jump in feet first!'

'Oh, yes – very funny, I don't think.'

Gramps finally managed to get Gareth's attention again. 'I gather I won't be able to try out that secret passage of yours,' he said.

''Fraid not. The tunnel's been put out of bounds.'

'I'm not at all happy about this whole business,' Gramps told him. 'The more I think about it, the less I like it. Is there any way I could get back into the Old Manor and speak to Taffy again?'

'That's the reason I'm ringing,' Gareth replied. 'We're competing against some local athletes tomorrow afternoon. If you were waiting nearby when they arrived – about two o'clock – you could follow them in through the gates.'

'Right, that's exactly what I'll do,' he promised. 'Take care, m'boy.'

'Will do, Gramps. See you then. Cheers!'

As Gareth switched off the phone, Adam tapped him on the arm.

'Hate to say this, GG, but we're not alone.'

Gareth looked round and saw Petit Pierre striding out of the trees towards them. He slipped the phone into the pocket of his tracksuit top, but feared that the coach might have already seen it.

The man walked right up to them before he spoke. 'What are you two doing here?' he asked, glancing down at Adam's wet jeans. 'As if I didn't know, Foxy.'

Adam saw no point in trying to deny the evidence. They had not yet had the chance to close the gap beneath the statue. Surprised by the use of his nickname, however, he decided to risk a direct question.

'Did you know about this tunnel, Coach?'

'Not until you people caused such a stir on Saturday,' he admitted with a grin.

Gareth suddenly realised that the coach was not speaking in his usual broken English. 'You're not really French, are you?' he said bravely.

'*Non*, but 'ow did you guess, *mon garçon?*' the man responded in a deliberately comic accent.

'So who are you?'

'Police. I'm Detective Inspector Robins and we're investigating what's going on here and at the Centre,' he told them. 'I came away from the house to make a call to the station, but my phone's gone dead. May I use yours?'

Chapter Ten
Over and Out

Next morning, Gareth was about to leave the changing room before the start of the training session when Blackbeard blocked his way.

'You've got a visitor, Davies,' the coach told him. 'Wait here.'

Puzzled, Gareth sat down on a bench, thinking Gramps must have arrived early and somehow bluffed his way in. When the door opened, he found Old Taffy staring at him with his piercing blue eyes, which were exactly the same as those of his young clone.

Gareth stood up and backed away nervously. 'What do you want with me?'

Taffy grinned. 'I want to make you a star!'

'A star?'

'That's right, boyo. Reckon that's the least I can do for the grandson of my old pal Davy.'

'And how are you going to do that?'

'Full of questions, ain't you? Just like Davy.'

'Well?'

'Well, for a start, we're going to take you away from here and…'

Gareth cut him off. 'I'm not going to that A.C.E. place so you can jab needles into me, if that's what you think.'

'That's exactly what I think,' Taffy said, making a move towards him. 'And you're going there right now.'

'I can't. Gramps is coming to see me today.'

Taffy was taken by surprise. 'Davy? He's coming back here?'

'You've got it. He wants to watch me in the high jump – and speak to you about things, too.'

'Things?'

'Yes, *things*,' Gareth stressed. 'You've got some explaining to do, Taffy Jones – and not just to Gramps…'

Taffy stared at him for a few moments, then turned and left the room.

The vintage Bentley purred past the chapel and pulled into a clump of trees, not far from the statue, letting the team bus disappear up the driveway. The automatic gates had closed so swiftly that they'd scraped the rear of the car as it squeezed through them after the bus.

Gramps had decided that it would be better not to park in the courtyard as he had done on Open Day, suspecting that they might not welcome such an early return visit – even if he wasn't quite sure who *they* might be.

He climbed out of the car to inspect the damage to its paintwork, shook his head, and then walked towards the lake to take another look at Taffy's statue.

'Had himself made to look like a Greek God,' he murmured. 'Typical!'

Gramps could not resist stepping on the stone discus, as he'd seen Adam do, and the front panel of the base rumbled forwards to reveal the open space beneath the statue.

'Huh!' he grunted. 'Perhaps just as well it's been flooded.'

He was about to close the gap when a movement among the trees caught his eye. His first instinct, perhaps a guilty echo from the past, was to hide somewhere, but then he recognised the figure slouching towards him.

'Fancy seeing you here again, Davy,' Taffy greeted him, but there was no offer of a handshake this time.

'Hello, Taffy,' said Gramps warily. 'Weren't expecting me, were you?'

'Well, young Gareth did let out that you might be back,' he admitted. 'I just wasn't sure if you'd be able to get in.'

'Get past them gates, you mean? Yes, they are a wee bit sharp.'

'Helps to keep out people who are not wanted,' Taffy told him.

'You including me in that?'

''Fraid so, Davy, old pal. It's a pity you were nosy enough to sneak back in.'

'Why? What's going on here that you want to keep such a secret?'

'More than you'll ever know.'

Gramps nodded. 'Including this cloning business, no doubt,' he said. 'Trying to play God. What did you hope to gain by that?'

'Immortality!' Taffy replied, grinning inanely. 'Taffy Jones will live on for ever!'

'You've gone mad.'

The grin faded and Taffy took a step forward, bunched his fist and then hit Gramps full in the face. The blow sent Gramps toppling backwards and, as he fell, his head struck the side of the stone plinth and he lay still.

Taffy looked at the crumpled body and gave a little sigh of regret. Then he took hold of the man's legs and began to drag him towards the yawning black hole.

'Goodbye, Davy,' he grunted with the effort. 'Sorry it had to end this way...'

'No sign of your grandad yet?' asked Tom.

Gareth shook his head. 'He was supposed to get here at the same time as this lot.'

As they watched the visiting athletes cross the courtyard towards the changing rooms, half a dozen burly men in blue tracksuits also left the bus and followed them.

'They've got more coaches than us,' muttered Adam. 'Speakin' of which, have you seen Petit Pierre today?'

'You mean D.I. Robins,' Eddie corrected.

'Yeah, right – have to start callin' him Robbo now instead!' Adam grinned. 'Still ain't sure Doubtin' Thomas here really believes it.'

Tom scowled. 'Not till he proves he's on our side.'

'Pity Old Taffy got warned about Gramps coming,' said Eddie. 'Wonder if he's done a runner and Robbo's gone after him?'

Gareth sighed. 'I just hope Gramps is OK.'

'Well, if you're worried,' said Adam, 'let's go and see if his car's somewhere. We've still got time.'

'The statue!' exclaimed Gareth. 'I bet he's gone there to have another look at it.'

The boys jogged off down the drive and reached the clearing near the statue just in time to see Taffy dragging a body along the ground.

'Hey!' shouted Adam, breaking into a sprint. 'Stop!'

'That's Gramps!' cried Gareth.

Startled by the boys' arrival, Taffy let go of his burden and drew a knife from his belt. 'Stay right where you are!' he commanded.

Adam carried on running, yelling threats at the top of his voice. He took off as if he were doing the long jump and flew through the air, feet first.

At the last moment, Taffy tried to sidestep the human missile, like a matador dodging a bull's charge, but he was too slow. The impact forced the breath from his body, sending the knife spiralling away, and Taffy crumpled to the ground, face down in the dirt.

Adam was winded, too, but Eddie arrived in time to jump on top of Taffy to try and stop him getting up again. Gareth had gone to attend to Gramps and was kneeling beside him, cradling the bleeding head in his lap.

'He's still alive!' he cried in relief. 'He's breathing!'

'Watch out!'

Tom's warning was in vain. Eddie failed to see Young Taffy dash out from the trees near the chapel and he was knocked sideways by the unexpected assault. The two boys rolled across the grass, grappling with one another, just as a group of blue-tracksuited men came running towards them, led by a man in black.

'Pierre's here!' cried Tom.

'Yeah, but who's this pair?' muttered Adam as two more men appeared from the opposite direction.

'About time you got here,' Old Taffy yelled at the bodyguards, who had halted 50 metres from the statue when they found themselves outnumbered. 'Do something!'

They did. They turned and fled, pursued by four of the armed police officers, who had been smuggled in on the local athletes' bus.

'Cowards!' screamed Young Taffy, who had broken free from Eddie's grip.

Old Taffy hauled himself stiffly to his feet in a last effort to assert his authority.

'You're just in the nick of time, Dubois,' he said, addressing his 'French' coach. 'These hooligans have attacked me. Take them away and lock them up somewhere till they can be dealt with.'

'It's you we've come to lock up, Jones,' came the calm reply. 'You're under arrest!'

'Arrest?' repeated Old Taffy, shocked. 'What on earth do you mean, Dubois?'

'I'll be asking the questions from now on, Jones. My name isn't Dubois. I am Detective Inspector Robins.'

As Old Taffy sank to his knees, head in hands, his clone seemed to give up, too. He went and knelt by the man's side, as if to comfort him, but then burst into tears. He suddenly seemed like an ordinary, frightened little boy.

'Keep both Taffys under armed guard back at the house while I call up some transport,' Robins told his two remaining officers. He bent over Gramps, who was beginning to stir. 'And we'll also need an ambulance for this poor chap.'

Chapter Eleven
Future Fortunes

'Uuuggghhh!' grunted Tom with the effort of launching the metal ball into the air.

As it plopped into the grass, he was forced to accept defeat in the shot-put event. 'Not good enough,' he admitted, shaking hands with the winner.

'Can't win 'em all,' the boy grinned. 'Don't be too greedy.'

Tom belched in response. He had celebrated his success in the discus by drinking a whole bottle of fruit juice in a single gulp, but he was now regretting that reckless act of bravado. 'Soz!' he said, rubbing his belly. 'Got a bit of gut-ache.'

The meeting with the local athletes had gone ahead, as planned, despite the drama by the lake. Gareth was absent from the high jump, having gone to the hospital with Gramps, but Adam reported for action in time to take part in the long-jump competition.

Still fired up with adrenalin after what had happened, Adam produced an enormous opening jump. He improved upon his personal best, and achieved his aim of breaking the B.A.S.E. Camp record. When the distance was announced, his raucous hoots of delight were heard right across the arena.

'Sounds like Foxy's enjoying himself,' chuckled Eddie, as he warmed up for his own event on the track, the 1,500-metre race.

The first two laps were too slow for Eddie's liking, little more than jogging pace, and he surged to the front along the back straight, increasing his lead with almost every stride.

'Go on, Wonder Boy!' Adam shouted as Eddie ran past the long-jump pit for the final time. 'Burn 'em up!'

Eddie flashed him a grin and changed gear again, proving he still had enough energy left for a fast finish, to claim a comfortable victory.

Adam and Tom went over to congratulate him and were soon joined by D.I. Robins. 'Well done to you all,' he said. 'You've had quite a day, one way and another.'

'Yeah, nobody's gonna beat my big jump,' Adam boasted.

'Your best jump was the one that flattened Old Taffy!' laughed Eddie.

The inspector smiled. 'All that remains to do now is something I've been looking forward to ever since I got here.'

'What's that?' said Tom.

'Arresting my ex-colleagues – including *Blackbeard*, as I believe you call him. He's the one who's really behind everything that goes on here.'

'When are you going to make the arrests?' asked Adam.

'Just as soon as the events are over and all the visitors have gone,' the inspector told them. 'We don't want to spoil everyone's fun, do we?'

Gareth returned from the hospital to find his friends wandering around the athletics track in the evening sunshine. They had been joined by Jacko, as both training camps had now been closed down, pending further investigations by the police.

'How's your gramps?' asked Eddie.

'He's going to be OK, thanks,' said Gareth. 'Still got a bit of a headache, though, so they're keeping him in overnight for observation.'

'We're all goin' home tomorrow,' said Adam. 'Most of the coaches were taken away in handcuffs this afternoon.'

'Including Blondie,' sighed Eddie. 'He's been really helpful to me. Good runner himself, too.'

'Well, he wasn't quick enough to escape the long arm of the law!' Tom grinned.

'Pity you missed seein' Blackbeard get bundled into the back of a van, GG,' Adam chuckled. 'That made my day.'

'Wonder what they'll do with the clone-kid?' said Tom, glancing at Jacko, who failed to react. He seemed almost in a state of shock at what had happened.

'Don't much care,' Eddie muttered, and then attempted a joke. 'YT might have to share another of Old Taffy's cells, if you get my meaning!'

The group reached the high-jump area and flopped onto one of the large cushions.

'Hope the camps will be opened up again some time,' said Adam. 'Y'know, they could be used by people trainin' for the Olympics and that in the future.'

Tom smirked. 'You mean people like you.'

'Yeah, people like me,' grinned Adam, before adding, 'and you lot as well!'

'So long as it is done right,' said Eddie. 'No drugs, no injections, no jungle-juices – and definitely no clones. What do you say, Jacko?'

He nodded in agreement. 'I knew it was all wrong really,' he admitted.

'Glad to hear you say that,' Eddie said with satisfaction.

Gareth bounced off the cushion, unable to keep the news to himself any longer. 'Foxy's not the only one who's had that idea,' he told them excitedly. 'Gramps is thinking about buying the Old Manor!'

'What!' Adam exclaimed. 'That bang on the head must be worse than they think. He's lost his marbles!'

Gareth grinned. 'No, he hasn't. Didn't I tell you – he's rich!'

The others looked at one another blankly.

'Think we might have remembered something like that,' said Tom.

'Sorry, I suppose we do tend to keep it quiet,' Gareth conceded. 'It can change the way people treat you, if they know.'

'Maybe Old Taffy *did* know,' said Adam. 'Perhaps he was gonna kidnap you and force Gramps to cough up loads of dosh.'

'Doubt it,' said Gareth. 'I mean, if that were the case, he wouldn't have tried to kill him, would he?'

'Hmm, you might have a point there,' Adam conceded.

'So is your gramps coming to live here?' asked Eddie.

Gareth shook his head. 'Don't think so, but I suppose he might come and stay every now and again. Y'know, keep an eye on the place, for old times' sake.'

'So what does he have planned?'

'Well, it's early days yet, of course, but there's enough space for coaching all kinds of sports, not just athletics. Football, rugby, cricket, gymnastics, swimming – you name it,' Gareth said, then added, 'and not just for boys.'

'Girls!' Adam grinned. 'Now that *would* be worth coming back here for!'

'Doubt if Taffy would agree to sell it to him,' said Tom. 'Not after what happened.'

'Yeah – guess that might be a problem,' Gareth admitted.

'What about YT?' Jacko put in. 'I don't suppose *he* will get locked up – he's too young, and it wasn't really his fault. Perhaps he deserves another chance.'

'Maybe that's how Gramps will persuade Old Taffy to sell up,' said Gareth. 'Y'know, if YT were allowed to live here and prove he can change his ways.'

'Hope so,' said Jacko. 'He's not a bad kid, really, once you get to know him.'

Gareth had done enough talking. 'Let's have a final jog around the track. Do a lap of honour!'

'You've *got* to be joking,' Tom protested, as everyone else jumped to their feet. 'I'm gonna turn in.'

'Oh no, you're not, Tom-Tom,' laughed Adam, steering him towards the track. 'I know what you've got in mind – sneakin' back inside for some more of that juice.'

'Juice is banned from now on,' Eddie told him. 'A bit of exercise will do you far more good.'

'Dead right!' agreed Gareth, breaking into a trot. 'You know, I reckon Gramps could be onto a great thing here – a real winner!'

'C'mon, guys, run!' cried Adam. 'Let's do it! Let's go for gold!'